BLOWN AWAY!

"This carving was the inspiration for my stories."
-Christine

ACKNOWLEDGMENTS

Thank you to my sister Angela Savard, for inspiring me to write my stories based on my carving.

Thank you Marcus Fregonese, my first greatest critic, inspiration and junior editor. He named Apollo, Juniper Eagle, Morris Squirrel and gave my story its appropriate final title.

Thank you Deb and Tony Grassi, my computer experts and patience-extraordinaire. A special thank you to Deb for countless hours in editing, proof-reading and contacting the right people to make this book a reality.

Thank you Glen Hawkes, for the entertaining and engaging illustrations that make my story appealing and come to life for all readers.

Thank you to all family members and friends who took the time to proof-read my stories.

Thank you Peter Shery, for giving Bizzee his voice and for bringing out The Woodland Characters' unique personalities in the Audiobooks.

Copyright © by Christine Soulliere 2022

All rights reserved. No part of this book may be used or reproduced in any manner whatsoever without prior written permission from the Author, except in the case of brief quotations embodied in critical articles and reviews.

ISBN 978-1-7779348-1-1

It has been three weeks since Bizzee Bear's airlift rescue. He looks physically fine and is as full of 'busyness' as ever. Everyday he enjoys fishing, foraging for food and playing with his woodland friends. Morris Squirrel, his close friend, challenges him to new heights. He's excelling. There was a time that Bizzee thought of himself as a scaredy-cat afraid of heights bear cub. Most of his friends thought he'd NEVER climb.

Well, 'never say never,' as his close friend Alexander Beetle always said.

Morris had suggested a doable rescue plan to get Bizzee Bear UNSTUCK from a very, very, tall birch tree. Unfortunately, during the whole event an unexpected fall led to other problems and lots of drama during and after the rescue.

Let's move on. Everyday, Bizzee Bear gains more courage with Morris' help and the young cub's activities lead him to venture farther into the forest. Today, Bizzee and two young raccoon friends, Rascal and Rowdy were exploring near Old Mill Road, which connects two small towns Eagles' Point and Crossover. This is a forbidden area for all the young, inexperienced woodland animals. All three friends had been warned NOT to travel in its direction. Mama Bear and Old Grandpa Raccoon were very specific about NEVER going more than two kilometres away from it. To ensure the youngsters knew the limit Mama Bear, Old Grandpa Raccoon and Grey Wolf, a friend, put specific scratch marks on the trees' trunks to act as markers. It took them days to complete the worthy task. The three curious friends ignored the warning and are close to Old Mill Road.

Earlier that day, Farmer Tom drove through the valley and crossed over to Old Mill Road. He whistled as he steered his dependable, rusty tractor pulling a wagon-load of the finest turnips money can buy, which he had purchased in Crossover. He chuckled as he imagined his pigs devouring them on cold, winter days. What made him even happier was the new Welsummer rooster that sat on top of his turnips. What a prize! As he rounded the curves in the road, Farmer Tom expertly avoided bumps and the deeper ruts to keep his load intact. He had just relaxed a bit when a sudden, unusual, strong gust of wind almost blew him off his tractor.

He quickly regained control of his tractor and stopped the swaying, over-loaded wagon from tipping. Little did he know, that his prize rooster had been BLOWN AWAY! As he drove along, he thought of the winning, blue ribbon rooster and was anxious to show it to his wife and hens. He knew the rooster would complete the hen house. To buy it, he and his wife Abigail had saved all their money from the sale of their fresh eggs and cream that they supplied to the town's only restaurant.

Abigail had seen a Welsummer rooster at the county fair and her heart was set on that particular breed. The previous owner, Farmer Wilson had never caged his rooster and had trained it to ride along with him wherever he went. So Farmer Tom followed suit.

When Abigail saw her husband coming toward the barn, she ran out to greet him and the new rooster. Tom and Abigail looked puzzled. They couldn't see or find it and searched the wagon and the yard. No rooster! What had happened to it? Tom looked at Abigail, scratched his head and recounted how a strong gust of wind had suddenly hit the tractor and wagon. He told her how busy he had been trying to manoeuver around the bumps and ruts and to control the tractor and wagon.

They both suspected what happened, jumped in their truck and drove at a snail's pace to search the sides of the road and its ditches for their rooster. After a long search the discouraged couple returned home.

The next day Farmer Tom and Abigail repeated the search and found nothing! Oh, they were so disappointed. They thought that someone may have found the lost rooster and claimed it as their own. Little did they know, that the strong gust of wind had blown their rooster much farther into the woods. It had survived the hurling and had landed in a prickly bush.

Bizzee Bear, Rascal and Rowdy Raccoon were in the area and witnessed the whole affair. They weren't sure how to approach the bird like animal stuck in the bush. They saw its feathers, two wings and two legs and figured it was some kind of bird. Cautiously, they moved closer. The dazed bird blinked its eyes and tried to untangle itself. Bizzee was the first to help. The freed bird was wobbly and could hardly walk.

"What are you?" Bizzee, Rascal and Rowdy asked timidly.

Not waiting for an answer, they introduced themselves. They saw that the strange, harmless bird needed their help.

"I'm a rooster," it informed them.

They had never seen a rooster and gave it their full attention and listened to it recount the day's events.

"I was sold to Farmer Tom, in a town called Crossover. We were headed to his farm near a new town, Eagles' Point. While travelling on Old Mill Road with his tractor and pulling a load of turnips, a strong unexpected gust of wind swept me up and blew me out of the wagon. With a quick forward motion it sent me into this prickly bush. The worst part is not knowing how to get to the farm from here.

Sooooooo.....I guess you can say that I'm LOST." "Can you help me get home?"inquired a sad rooster.

The woodland friends did not know Farmer Tom. They had never heard of or seen Crossover or Eagles' Point and they had no idea what a tractor or a wagon load of turnips were. Bizzee Bear, Rascal and Rowdy Raccoon were afraid to admit to this poor, lost rooster that they were in a forbidden part of the forest and they weren't too sure how to help him. They were shocked to learn that this rooster with such beautiful, large feathers and wings, can't fly. Because they knew about the forests' dangers they strongly suggested that he team up with them for his own protection from hungry predators.

The rooster hesitated. The only animals he knew lived on farms. His previous owner, Farmer Wilson, had provided and cared for him. He had been gentle and kind. The rooster hadn't gotten to know Farmer Tom but figured that anyone who whistled while driving an old tractor on a bumpy road with deep ruts must be an easygoing person. He was looking forward to living on his farm.

Bizzee, Rascal, and Rowdy understood how the rooster felt and promised to get him home safely. They told him about Alexander Beetle and Morris Squirrel, two excellent problem solvers that are always ready and willing to help others.

"I'll go with you. I feel safe with all three of you. Please call me Nester." Encouraged by his decision, he smiled and asked them to repeat their names.

"No problem, I'm Bizzee Bear. My mother says I was born busy and I'm too curious for my own good."

"I'm Rascal Raccoon. My grandpa says I'm mischievous and a fast climber."

"I'm Rowdy Raccoon. Grandpa Raccoon says I take after my dad; brave and always looking for new adventures."

Nester felt their kindness and followed them. As Bizzee led the way, the rooster wondered if he would ever get to Farmer Tom's. After a long time walking through the tall grass, he felt very tired. He wished that he was better at dodging the low overhanging branches that snagged his feathers.

Bizzee Bear offered to let him ride on his back as long as he crouched close to him and held on tight.

"No problem with riding as long as a sudden gust of wind doesn't blow me away," laughed a relieved rooster and he hopped up onto the cub's back.

After experiencing such an eventful day, the three friends appreciated Nester's sense of humour. They knew he would fit in with all of their woodland friends.

Bizzee, Rascal, Rowdy and Nester travelled at a good pace for an hour. Suddenly, the animals stopped and crouched as low as they could and hid under a protective spruce. No one made a sound. No one moved. Nester didn't dare ask what was going on.

He scrunched deeper into Bizzee's thick, furry back. Something was approaching and it stopped where they were hiding. The intruder dared to come closer. They adopted their new strategy and teamwork mode and lunged at the unknown creature. Bizzee, Rascal and Rowdy never left the protective tree while defending themselves. Nester clung to Bizzee's back. Their attacker was the same cougar who had tried to have their grandpa raccoon for dinner a few weeks ago. Because of the force of the surprise attack, Snarly Cougar suspected that he was facing a very large enemy. After much snarling, hissing, and biting throughout the attack, Snarly gave up the fight and ran off into another part of the forest.

"That was close!" murmured Bizzee Bear.

"Too close for comfort," added a frightened Rascal Raccoon. "I'm glad we practised a surprise attack plan before venturing out this way. The strategy really worked."

"It did this time," added an unsure Rowdy Raccoon licking his aching paw.

Nester stayed curled up and didn't dare move a feather or bat an eye. The three friends reassured him that Snarly Cougar had moved to another part of the forest and they continued their journey.
Nester tried to relax.

The four friends didn't travel too far before they spotted an opossum family. The mother was carrying her youngsters in her pouch and on her back. Bizzee explained that opossums feed at night, live mostly in trees and that the mother isn't a threat to them. If she is caught by an enemy she'll roll up into a ball and pretend she's dead to confuse it and hopefully get away.

Moving along as quiet as little mice, the woodland friends walked cautiously past rock piles, small caves and huge hollow logs. Disturbing a fox or vixen who fiercely protected their kits would not be wise.

As the sun set the interior of the forest grew darker. The occasional chatter of other animals scared Nester. He recognized barnyard voices but these sounds were strange. He longed for country rides in a wagon or truck. He wanted to eat corn and wheat and top off the food with a cool drink of water. He hadn't had a drink since early morning. He missed the simpler and quieter farm life. The forest suited his new companions and he saw how they coped with its challenges.

The quiet signal was given again. They stopped. A bobcat and a porcupine were about to cross paths and were staring intently at each other. They challenged each other. The porcupine had the advantage and the bobcat backed away to avoid sharp quills in his face and legs.

"Because porcupines can live up to ten years these two enemies will cross paths again," explained Rascal and he stated that they NEVER disturb a porcupine.

As Rascal and Rowdy got closer to their home, they raced each other to the stream for a cool drink and a swim. They had been without water all day.

Bizzee Bear picked up the pace, too. Nester hung on tightly. As he bounced up and down he was reminded of the county fair's rodeo horses and their riders. He enjoyed every minute of it.

At the stream, Nester Rooster was forgotten and the thirsty cub dove headfirst into the water. He enjoyed a long drink then noticed the struggling rooster and realized that he was NOT a waterbird and could not swim nor float. He pushed Nester's waterlogged body onto the shore.

"Well that was refreshing," said Nester coughing and gasping for air. "Now I know why I've never been too fond of Farmer Wilson's pond." He tried to laugh to cover up his fright.

"Sorry about dunking you. You're so light that I forgot you were on my back," expressed an apologetic cub.

"You're a good sport," agreed the frolicking raccoons. In no time at all, Nester's feathers were dried and preened. He was tired and wanted a soft place to rest.

Bizzee, Rascal and Rowdy had family business to attend to before Nester could settle down for the night. An explanation of their day's whereabouts was expected and they were not in a hurry to face their parents. They quickly introduced Nester and explained how they found and helped him travel safely through the forest. They hoped his story would help them plead their case. Well it did and it didn't. After a few promises and negotiations the three friends were still allowed to visit each other, but their adventures were restricted. CLOSE TO HOME ONLY!!! The bargain suited them for now.

They found a few things that Nester could eat and asked Rubee Rabbit to share her log with him for the night. Neither Rubee nor Nester minded. After eating a bit more and drinking from the stream Nester said goodnight to everyone.

The night passed quietly and uneventfully.

Usually, woodland animals wake up on their own and at their own time. Nester was about to change their routines. Promptly at sunrise, he walked out of Rubee Rabbit's cozy log, strutted about and crowed. His voice was louder and more energetic than usual.

"Must be all the fresh air," he murmured as he walked with great exaggerated steps and crowed a loud COCK-A-DOODLE-DOOOO.

Rubee Rabbit looked strangely at him and folded her ears to block out the piercing sound.

"Good morning Rubee. COCK-A- DOODLE-DOO, COCK-A-DOODLEDOO, COCK-A DOODLE-DOO."

Rubee Rabbit wasn't sure what to say or do.

Many animals ran to her home to investigate the earsplitting noise. First to arrive, was a very agitated Lester Chipmunk. He shook so much that he couldn't speak. Nester introduced himself and explained that he was a rooster and how he always crowed every morning at sunrise.

"I'm sure we'll adjust to it in time," uttered a polite and calmer chipmunk.

As other animals approached, they marvelled at Nester's colourful feathers and couldn't believe he had made such high pitched sounds.

Nester puffed up his chest to crow again but stopped when many animals covered their ears. Their actions confused him. No one had ever disliked his cock-a-doodle-ing before.

Curious, Hector Mouse, Sister Bear and Goldie Canary introduced themselves and admired Nester's extraordinary plumage. Sister Bear told him where he could find the best berries to eat. Nester nodded to her and smiled even though he was not sure if they would be as good as his usual corn and wheat. Feeling a little adventurous he promised to give them a try. Splash Frog hopped along on the shore just as Nester stopped at the stream. Splash eyed him suspiciously. He didn't want to be someone's breakfast. At that moment his friends Bizzee Bear, Rascal and Rowdy Raccoon gathered around. Bizzee explained Nester's situation and how he needed everyone's input to come up with a solution to get him home.

"Have you talked to Morris Squirrel or Alexander Beetle yet?" yelled Splash from his favourite rock.

"Nester was too tired last night," replied Bizzee.

Next, Bizzee led Nester to the tall, birch tree where Alexander Beetle lived. When Alexander saw Nester, his feelers vibrated and his spots rotated and if you listened carefully you could hear little sounds coming from them. He was thinking and was momentarily at a loss for words.

His voice squeaked, "A-re y-y-you a Wel-Wel -summer rooster? I've seen pictures of your breed. Your plumage is so bright and colourful. Your comb is as red as the pictures in the county magazines. You are a blue, ribbon winner at the county fairs. You are ..."

Bizzee Bear coughed to get Alexander Beetle's attention and to stop him from sharing everything he knew about Welsummer roosters. He could talk for hours and always impressed everyone with his knowledge of so many things. Bizzee counted on Alexander's expertise to get this rooster, that could neither fly nor swim and was not suited to walk through the forest, home. Alexander adopted a serious mode and asked the animals present if they had heard of Crossover or Eagles' Point. They all answered no.

Goldie Canary thought of Apollo and Juniper, the Rock Hill Forest eagles, and wondered if they had visited these towns. She told everyone to pass the word along that the eagles were needed under the tall birch. Her message got everyone's attention and they shared what they knew and how they felt about travelling to unknown towns.

Mama and Papa Elk answered that they had never seen or heard of Eagles' Point and would never travel there. They enjoyed their present lifestyle and were satisfied to stay in this part of the forest.

Due to his age Maximilian Moose stated that he had not been to Eagles' Point and didn't care to travel too far. Long journeys did not appeal to him at this time.

Mama Bear was all for travelling out of this area and to experience new adventures but she had never considered it while raising cubs. Eagles' Point caught her interest and she hoped to see it some day.

Old Grandpa Raccoon occasionally wandered near Old Mill Road but never crossed it.

Grey Wolf was out hunting and didn't get the message.

When Morris Squirrel arrived, he apologized for not getting there sooner. All the animals cried out, "We know, it was Tuesday and at three o'clock you always have a prior commitment!"

Morris laughed. He understood that they were teasing him... in a nice way. He met Nester Rooster and heard about his dilemma. He immediately suggested airlifting him home because he couldn't fly and was not suited to walk through the thick forest.

"Apollo and Juniper are the answer," shouted all the animals. "They are equipped to do the task and have plenty of experience. "They looked at Bizzee and smiled.

Alexander Beetle agreed that it could be an easy plan to carry out and the rooster's weight would not be a problem during the flight. Alexander was still thinking about this plan when his feelers started to vibrate and his spots rotated and if you listened hard enough you could hear little sounds coming from them. A different idea was forming in his mind and he asked if anyone had ever heard of a hot air balloon. He continued telling them that it was an ideal way to travel from place to place and it was done in the air. He quickly drew a picture of it in the sandy soil. The animals visualized what he was talking about.

"Who will build this contraption?" inquired a doubtful Maximilian Moose.

"Where will we get the materials to build it?" asked an anxious Rowdy Raccoon.

"Its fire can get out of control and burn our forest," shouted a very worried Lester Chipmunk.

"What if the balloon develops a hole?" added Old Grandpa Raccoon.

"Who will navigate this flying thingeee?" laughed an excited Splash Frog.

"What if a strong gust of wind blows me off course?" asked a nervous Nester Rooster.

The animals agreed to put Alexander's idea on hold until the eagles had some input. Everyone decided to think about it some more, and they left to go to bed. Alexander continued mumbling about its possibilities as he climbed to his nest.

Early the next morning, Nester woke up with a burst of energy. He had to greet the beautiful sunrise with a loud crowing voice. He knew some of the woodland animals objected to it but it was the only way he could show them how he felt about their friendships and the great sunny day.

"I'm a rooster. I crow. That's what I do. How else can I show them how appreciative I am for everything they've done and what they'll be doing to help get me home?"

Using a softer voice he started his cock-a-doodle-ing. His lungs filled with more air and he bellowed the next COCK-A-DOODLE-DOO. Bizzee anticipated Nester's crowing and was right beside him to muffle it because some of the animals could get pretty cranky if their early morning sleep was disturbed. He wanted everybody in a happy, helpful mood.

At nine o'clock the eagles flew in and they met Nester Rooster.

At first Nester was intimidated by their sharp talons and beaks but he soon felt some familiarity toward them and decided to TRUST them.

The eagles listened to Nester's story and realized how much he wanted to find his way home. They told Goldie and the others that they had flown over both towns but didn't recall seeing Tom and Abigail's farm. The eagles listened to both plans that Morris Squirrel and Alexander suggested.

Not wanting to discourage Alexander's creative and helpful ideas, the eagles agreed that the hot air balloon was doable but would require too much time to build and to test. Nester needed transportation home to his owners as soon as the farm was located. As they talked Juniper whispered something to Apollo. They both excused themselves and promised to be back within an hour or two.

"That's strange," thought the animals.

"They are acting a little secretive. It must be an emergency of some kind. Why else would they leave?" explained Mama Bear.

Some animals decided to go about their own business and to return later.

Bizzee Bear took this time to show Nester Rooster the tall, birch tree where he had had his first climb and he talked about the events that took place there, during and after it. As Nester listened it amazed him how inventive and helpful each animal can be in a crisis.

"Show me how high you can climb," expressed a very, excited rooster.

As Bizzee made his way up he recalled his first climb, the breathtaking view and the true friendships shown by his friends. He waved to Nester and felt so proud that he could climb.

"That was amazing!" Nester was so happy for Bizzee that he wanted to crow out the biggest cock-a-doodle-doo. He puffed up his chest and let out a long breath but just made little cackling sounds and whispered to Bizzee, "I do not want to disturb anyone."

Bizzee just shook his head and ruffled Nester's feathers.

The animals gathered around again after an hour. Apollo and Juniper swooped down near Nester and handed him a scrunched paper.

"Is this you and Farmer Tom?" they asked.

"Yes it is. Where did you get this picture? I remember the photographer taking it of us in Crossover the day I was bought," answered an excited rooster.

"Well that farmer and his wife can't wait to get you back. They have similar posters along Old Mill Road asking for your return-- if found. We scouted the area near Eagles' Point many times before spotting their names on their barn. We shrieked and circled their farm several times to get their attention. Farmer Tom, who had been milking his cow, walked out of the barn carrying a pail of milk and looked up to find out what was shrieking. Abigail ran out of the house and joined him. Together, they scanned the sky and spotted us landing on the load of turnips. They looked frightened and confused. Approaching cautiously, they saw their scrunched poster held under our feet. We continued to peck at it over and over again until Tom and Abigail nodded. They seemed to understand that we had seen their precious rooster. Communication was difficult but with many more gestures they got the message that we had you. Both Tom and Abigail didn't understand when or how you'll be returned to them. We think they will meet us at the load of turnips as soon as they hear any strange sounds or see movements in the sky or on their road. We've never seen such a happy couple. You are such a prize rooster that they never expected anyone to return you. We plan to drop you off tomorrow morning. That will give everyone a chance to say goodbye tonight. Now, we must go hunt for food to feed our eaglets. We'll see you in the morning."

Before they left they teased Maximilian and asked him if he had done any donkey-kick fishing lately. The animals smiled. Maximilian just grunted.

All the woodland animals seemed pleased that the farm was located and that the farmers were anxious to receive their prize rooster.

Even though the woodland animals had just met Nester Rooster a few days ago they found him interesting and knew that they would miss him. Some animals admitted that they would also miss his SOFT cock-adoodle-doos at sunrise. They questioned him about farm animals, county fairs, winning blue ribbons, crowing contests, other kinds of roosters, riding in wagons and trucks and especially his adventure through the forest with Bizzee, Rascal and Rowdy. They were impressed that Nester led such a different life in the country and experienced so many things.

Alexander wanted a celebrity send off for the notable Nester and presented him with a chain of wild flowers that he and Morris had created. Nester wore it proudly and started to make great exaggerated steps, puffed up his chest, and... Rubee Rabbit quickly folded her ears and the other animals did the same before Nester bellowed three, shrill and happy cock-a-doodle-doos and bowed gracefully and grandly. The animals clapped.

Rascal and Rowdy jumped onto Splash's rock and began their usual happy dance. Soon all the woodland animals, as well as the Elk family from the meadow, joined in the dancing.

Grey Wolf, who had been away for several days, enjoyed hearing all about Bizzee's and the raccoon brother's latest adventure. He was thankful that the eagles were able to find Nester's owners and he joined in the celebration and danced too. Soon everyone agreed that it was time to say good night.

Nester was too excited to sleep and spent some time alone with Bizzee before joining Rubee Rabbit in her cozy home. He listened to the forest's night sounds and said he would miss some of them.

At sunrise Nester was doing his morning ritual of taking exaggerated steps and puffing up his chest to begin his cock-a-doodle-ing when one by one the animals surprised him and surrounded him to listen to his crowing without covering their ears. He felt so proud and crowed three more times COCK-A-DOODLE-DOO, COCK-A-DOODLE-DOO, COCK-ADOODLE-DOO. They cheered, clapped and stamped their feet.

The eagles arrived and all of the animals greeted and thanked them.

"Operation airlift will be in progress in three minutes," announced Apollo seriously.

Nester thanked everyone for their hospitality. He walked over to Bizzee, Rascal and Rowdy and thanked them once again for rescuing him and for sharing all their friends. He told Morris and Alexander that he trusted the airlift plan and Apollo and Juniper to carry it out.

"Well, up, up and away everybody! Hopefully no gust of wind will interfere with our flight," said an excited rooster.

Nester crouched, tucked in his head, wings and legs and was ready to be swept up by Juniper. Apollo would fly by their side. All the woodland animals started the count down... 10,9,8,7,6,5,4,3,2,1 and shouted, "Lift off!"

Because Nester's head was tucked under his wing and he couldn't see what it was like below him, he used his imagination. He thought of tree tops, the stream that ran through Rock Hill Forest and Mama Bear and her cubs fishing in it, a fox waiting on a hillside and the elk family grazing in the valley. He felt the wind currents from the eagles' wings and the cooler air. He thought about open fields, tractors and wagons, horses and cattle, ducks and chickens. Lots of chickens. He wondered what Abigail would be like and was anxious to see Farmer Tom again.

Nester could feel himself descending and heard familiar sounds and smelled turnips as Juniper soft landed him. He unfolded his head and opened his eyes and heard Farmer Tom's familiar voice as he introduced Nester to his wife, Abigail. Farmer Tom and Abigail laughed and cried as they held him and gently squeezed him. They saw that he was very healthy and had only minor scratches on his back.

Using hand and facial gestures Abigail tried to thank the eagles and to tell them that they were welcome to visit at anytime. Before they left they celebrated with plenty of food and water and enjoyed Farmer Tom's fiddling. Nester was introduced to his new barnyard friends. All the familiar sounds were heard and recognized; even the cat's. And Nester knew that he was home.

The hens were the most excited and showed the eagles how grateful they were by performing the famous chicken dance in their honour. They danced and cackled as Nester bid good-bye to the eagles and he invited them to visit the little farm at anytime, even as early as sunrise. They promised to drop in.

That night a very excited and tired rooster settled in his new hen house and dreamed of his woodland friends in the light of the full, country moon.

Meanwhile, the woodland friends continued sharing stories of their short time with Nester and vowed to get up at SUNRISE to hear Nester's crowing carried by a strong gust of wind blowing their way. Cock-a-doodle-doo, ... cock-a-doodle-do, ... cock-a-doodle-dooooooo ... to you my Rock Hill Forest friends.

The Woodland Adventures

OTHER ADVENTURES

Enjoy more exciting adventures with Bizzee Bear and his friends in the next books of The Woodland Adventures Series:

The Woodland Adventures Book 3: Can Rock Hill Forest Be Saved?

The Woodland Adventures Book 4: Forever Committed

The Woodland Adventures Book 5: Alexander's Big Surprise

The Woodland Adventures Book 1: *The Great Birch Climb*, available at Amazon.ca

Audio Books of *The Great Birch Climb* & *Blown Away*   AVAILABLE ON ▶ YouTube

This Cookbook Belongs To

_____

Enjoying this cookbook?

Please leave a review because we would love to hear your feedback, opinions and advice to create better products and services for you! Also, we want to know how you creatively use your notebooks and journals.

Thank you for your support.
You are greatly appreciated!

BlankPublishers

Copyright © 2018 All Rights Reserved

BAKING JOURNAL

Recipe	Page

BAKING JOURNAL

Recipe   Page

BAKING JOURNAL

Recipe   Page

BAKING JOURNAL

Recipe	Page

Recipe Name: _____

Serves: _____ Cook Time: _____

Ingredients Directions

_____

_____

_____

_____

_____

_____

_____

_____

_____

_____

_____

_____

Notes:

Page:

Recipe Name: _____

Serves: _____ Cook Time: _____

Ingredients _____ Directions _____

_____
_____
_____
_____
_____
_____
_____
_____
_____
_____
_____
_____
_____

Notes:

Page:

Recipe Name: _____

Serves: _____   Cook Time: _____

Ingredients _____   Directions _____

Notes:

Page:

Recipe Name:_____

Serves:_____   Cook Time:_____

Ingredients_____   Directions_____

_____
_____
_____
_____
_____
_____
_____
_____
_____
_____
_____
_____
_____
_____

Notes:

Page:

Recipe Name: _____

Serves: _____   Cook Time: _____

Ingredients _____   Directions _____

_____
_____
_____
_____
_____
_____
_____
_____
_____
_____
_____
_____
_____
_____

Notes:

Page:

Recipe Name: _____

Serves: _____   Cook Time: _____

Ingredients _____   Directions _____

_____
_____
_____
_____
_____
_____
_____
_____
_____
_____
_____
_____
_____
_____

Notes:

Page:

Recipe Name: _____

Serves: _____   Cook Time: _____

Ingredients   Directions
_____   _____
_____   _____
_____   _____
_____   _____
_____   _____
_____   _____
_____   _____
_____   _____
_____   _____
_____   _____
_____   _____
_____   _____

Notes:

Page:

Recipe Name: _____

Serves: _____   Cook Time: _____

Ingredients _____ Directions _____

_____
_____
_____
_____
_____
_____
_____
_____
_____
_____
_____
_____
_____
_____

Notes:

Page:

Recipe Name:_____

Serves:_____   Cook Time:_____

Ingredients   Directions
_____   _____

_____   _____

_____   _____

_____   _____

_____   _____

_____   _____

_____   _____

_____   _____

_____   _____

_____   _____

_____   _____

_____   _____

Notes:

Page:

Recipe Name:_____

Serves:_____ Cook Time:_____

Ingredients_____ Directions_____

Notes:

Page:

Recipe Name: _____

Serves: _____   Cook Time: _____

Ingredients   Directions
_____
_____
_____
_____
_____
_____
_____
_____
_____
_____
_____
_____
_____
_____

Notes:

Page:

Recipe Name: _____

Serves: _____   Cook Time: _____

Ingredients   Directions
_____
_____
_____
_____
_____
_____
_____
_____
_____
_____
_____
_____
_____
_____

Notes:

Page:

Recipe Name:_____

Serves: _____ Cook Time: _____

Ingredients _____ Directions _____

Notes:

Page:

Recipe Name: _____

Serves: _____ Cook Time: _____

Ingredients Directions
_____
_____
_____
_____
_____
_____
_____
_____
_____
_____
_____
_____
_____

Notes:

Page:

Recipe Name: _____

Serves: _____ Cook Time: _____

Ingredients _____ Directions _____

_____
_____
_____
_____
_____
_____
_____
_____
_____
_____
_____
_____
_____
_____

Notes:

Page:

Recipe Name: _____

Serves: _____ Cook Time: _____

Ingredients _____ Directions _____

_____
_____
_____
_____
_____
_____
_____
_____
_____
_____
_____
_____
_____

Notes:

Page:

Recipe Name:_____

Serves:_____ Cook Time:_____

Ingredients   Directions

_____

_____

_____

_____

_____

_____

_____

_____

_____

_____

_____

_____

_____

_____

Notes:

Page:

Recipe Name: _____

Serves: _____   Cook Time: _____

Ingredients _____   Directions _____

_____

_____

_____

_____

_____

_____

_____

_____

_____

_____

_____

_____

Notes:

Page:

Recipe Name:_____

Serves: _____   Cook Time: _____

Ingredients _____   Directions _____

_____
_____
_____
_____
_____
_____
_____
_____
_____
_____
_____
_____
_____
_____

Notes:

Page:

Recipe Name: _____

Serves: _____ Cook Time: _____

Ingredients _____ Directions _____

Notes:

Page:

Recipe Name:_____

Serves:_____   Cook Time:_____

Ingredients   Directions

_____
_____
_____
_____
_____
_____
_____
_____
_____
_____
_____
_____
_____
_____

Notes:

Page:

Recipe Name: _____

Serves: _____ Cook Time: _____

Ingredients _____ Directions _____

_____
_____
_____
_____
_____
_____
_____
_____
_____
_____
_____
_____
_____

Notes:

Page:

Recipe Name: _____

Serves: _____   Cook Time: _____

Ingredients _____   Directions _____

_____

_____

_____

_____

_____

_____

_____

_____

_____

_____

_____

_____

_____

_____

Notes:

Page:

Recipe Name: _____

Serves: _____ Cook Time: _____

Ingredients _____ Directions _____

_____

_____

_____

_____

_____

_____

_____

_____

_____

_____

_____

_____

_____

Notes:

Page:

Recipe Name:_____

Serves:_____ Cook Time:_____

Ingredients_____ Directions_____

_____
_____
_____
_____
_____
_____
_____
_____
_____
_____
_____
_____
_____

Notes:

Page:

Recipe Name: _____

Serves: _____ Cook Time: _____

Ingredients _____ Directions _____

_____

_____

_____

_____

_____

_____

_____

_____

_____

_____

_____

_____

_____

Notes:

Page:

Recipe Name: _____

Serves: _____ Cook Time: _____

Ingredients Directions

_____
_____
_____
_____
_____
_____
_____
_____
_____
_____
_____
_____
_____
_____

Notes:

Page:

Recipe Name: _____

Serves: _____ Cook Time: _____

Ingredients _____ Directions _____

Notes:

Page:

Recipe Name:_____

Serves:_____   Cook Time:_____

Ingredients_____   Directions_____

_____
_____
_____
_____
_____
_____
_____
_____
_____
_____
_____
_____
_____
_____

Notes:

Page:

Recipe Name:_____

Serves:_____ Cook Time:_____

Ingredients_____ Directions_____

_____
_____
_____
_____
_____
_____
_____
_____
_____
_____
_____
_____
_____

Notes:

Page:

Recipe Name:_____

Serves:_____ Cook Time:_____

Ingredients   Directions

_____
_____
_____
_____
_____
_____
_____
_____
_____
_____
_____
_____

Notes:

Page:

Recipe Name: _____

Serves: _____   Cook Time: _____

Ingredients _____   Directions _____

_____
_____
_____
_____
_____
_____
_____
_____
_____
_____
_____
_____

Notes:

Page:

Recipe Name: _____

Serves: _____   Cook Time: _____

Ingredients   Directions

Notes:

Page:

Recipe Name: _____

Serves: _____ Cook Time: _____

Ingredients _____ Directions _____

Notes:

Page:

Recipe Name:_____

Serves:_____   Cook Time:_____

Ingredients   Directions
_____
_____
_____
_____
_____
_____
_____
_____
_____
_____
_____
_____
_____
_____

Notes:

Page:

Recipe Name: _____

Serves: _____ Cook Time: _____

Ingredients _____ Directions _____

Notes:

Page:

Recipe Name: _____

Serves: _____   Cook Time: _____

Ingredients   Directions

_____   _____

_____   _____

_____   _____

_____   _____

_____   _____

_____   _____

_____   _____

_____   _____

_____   _____

_____   _____

_____   _____

_____   _____

Notes:

Page:

Recipe Name: _____

Serves: _____ Cook Time: _____

Ingredients _____ Directions _____

_____

_____

_____

_____

_____

_____

_____

_____

_____

_____

_____

_____

_____

Notes:

Page:

Recipe Name: _____

Serves: _____ Cook Time: _____

Ingredients _____ Directions _____

_____

_____

_____

_____

_____

_____

_____

_____

_____

_____

_____

_____

Notes:

Page:

Recipe Name:_____

Serves:_____ Cook Time:_____

Ingredients_____ Directions_____

Notes:

Page:

Recipe Name: _____

Serves: _____   Cook Time: _____

Ingredients   Directions

_____

_____

_____

_____

_____

_____

_____

_____

_____

_____

_____

_____

_____

Notes:

Page:

Recipe Name: _____

Serves: _____   Cook Time: _____

Ingredients _____   Directions _____

_____

_____

_____

_____

_____

_____

_____

_____

_____

_____

_____

_____

Notes:

Page:

Recipe Name: _____

Serves: _____   Cook Time: _____

Ingredients _____   Directions _____

_____

_____

_____

_____

_____

_____

_____

_____

_____

_____

_____

_____

_____

_____

Notes:

Page:

Recipe Name:_____

Serves:_____ Cook Time:_____

Ingredients   Directions

_____
_____
_____
_____
_____
_____
_____
_____
_____
_____
_____
_____

Notes:

Page:

Recipe Name: _____

Serves: _____ Cook Time: _____

Ingredients Directions

_____

_____

_____

_____

_____

_____

_____

_____

_____

_____

_____

_____

_____

_____

Notes:

Page:

Recipe Name: _____

Serves: _____ Cook Time: _____

Ingredients _____ Directions _____

_____
_____
_____
_____
_____
_____
_____
_____
_____
_____
_____
_____

Notes:

Page:

Recipe Name: _____

Serves: _____ Cook Time: _____

Ingredients	Directions

Notes:

Page:

Recipe Name:_____

Serves:_____   Cook Time:_____

Ingredients_____   Directions_____

_____
_____
_____
_____
_____
_____
_____
_____
_____
_____
_____
_____

Notes:

Page:

Recipe Name:_____

Serves:_____   Cook Time:_____

Ingredients_____   Directions_____

_____
_____
_____
_____
_____
_____
_____
_____
_____
_____
_____
_____
_____

Notes:

Page:

Recipe Name:_____

Serves: _____ Cook Time: _____

Ingredients _____ Directions _____

_____
_____
_____
_____
_____
_____
_____
_____
_____
_____
_____
_____
_____

Notes:

Page:

Recipe Name: _____

Serves: _____ Cook Time: _____

Ingredients _____ Directions _____

_____

_____

_____

_____

_____

_____

_____

_____

_____

_____

_____

_____

_____

_____

Notes:

Page:

Recipe Name: _____

Serves: _____ Cook Time: _____

Ingredients   Directions

Notes:

Page:

Recipe Name:_____

Serves: _____ Cook Time: _____

Ingredients _____ Directions _____

_____

_____

_____

_____

_____

_____

_____

_____

_____

_____

_____

_____

_____

_____

Notes:

Page:

Recipe Name: _____

Serves: _____   Cook Time: _____

Ingredients _____   Directions _____

_____

_____

_____

_____

_____

_____

_____

_____

_____

_____

_____

_____

Notes:

Page:

Recipe Name:_____

Serves: _____ Cook Time: _____

Ingredients _____ Directions _____

_____

_____

_____

_____

_____

_____

_____

_____

_____

_____

_____

_____

_____

Notes:

Page:

Recipe Name:_____

Serves:_____   Cook Time:_____

Ingredients_____   Directions_____

_____
_____
_____
_____
_____
_____
_____
_____
_____
_____
_____
_____
_____

Notes:

Page:

Recipe Name:_____

Serves:_____ Cook Time:_____

Ingredients   Directions
_____
_____
_____
_____
_____
_____
_____
_____
_____
_____
_____
_____
_____
_____
_____
_____

Notes:

Page:

Recipe Name: _____

Serves: _____   Cook Time: _____

Ingredients _____   Directions _____

_____

_____

_____

_____

_____

_____

_____

_____

_____

_____

_____

_____

Notes:

Page:

Recipe Name: _____

Serves: _____   Cook Time: _____

Ingredients   Directions

_____
_____
_____
_____
_____
_____
_____
_____
_____
_____
_____
_____
_____
_____

Notes:

Page:

Recipe Name:_____

Serves:_____ Cook Time:_____

Ingredients   Directions
_____
_____
_____
_____
_____
_____
_____
_____
_____
_____
_____
_____
_____

Notes:

Page:

Recipe Name: _____

Serves: _____   Cook Time: _____

Ingredients   Directions

Notes:

Page:

Recipe Name: _____

Serves: _____   Cook Time: _____

Ingredients _____   Directions _____

Notes:

Page:

Recipe Name: _____

Serves: _____ Cook Time: _____

Ingredients Directions

Notes:

Page:

Recipe Name: _____

Serves: _____   Cook Time: _____

Ingredients   Directions
_____
_____
_____
_____
_____
_____
_____
_____
_____
_____
_____
_____

Notes:

Page:

Recipe Name: _____

Serves: _____ Cook Time: _____

Ingredients _____ Directions _____

_____
_____
_____
_____
_____
_____
_____
_____
_____
_____
_____
_____
_____

Notes:

Page:

Recipe Name:_____

Serves:_____ Cook Time:_____

Ingredients_____ Directions_____

Notes:

Page:

Recipe Name: _____

Serves: _____ Cook Time: _____

Ingredients Directions
_____
_____
_____
_____
_____
_____
_____
_____
_____
_____
_____
_____
_____
_____

Notes:

Page:

Recipe Name:_____

Serves:_____ Cook Time:_____

Ingredients   Directions

Notes:

Page:

Recipe Name:_____

Serves:_____ Cook Time:_____

Ingredients   Directions
_____
_____
_____
_____
_____
_____
_____
_____
_____
_____
_____
_____
_____
_____

Notes:

Page:

Recipe Name: _____

Serves: _____   Cook Time: _____

Ingredients   Directions
_____
_____
_____
_____
_____
_____
_____
_____
_____
_____
_____
_____
_____

Notes:

Page:

Recipe Name: _____

Serves: _____ Cook Time: _____

Ingredients _____ Directions _____

Notes:

Page:

Recipe Name:_____

Serves:_____ Cook Time:_____

Ingredients_____ Directions_____

_____
_____
_____
_____
_____
_____
_____
_____
_____
_____
_____
_____
_____
_____

Notes:

Page:

Recipe Name: _____

Serves: _____ Cook Time: _____

Ingredients _____ Directions _____

_____
_____
_____
_____
_____
_____
_____
_____
_____
_____
_____
_____
_____
_____

Notes:

Page:

Recipe Name: _____

Serves: _____ Cook Time: _____

Ingredients   Directions

Notes:

Page:

Recipe Name:_____

Serves:_____ Cook Time:_____

Ingredients   Directions
_____
_____
_____
_____
_____
_____
_____
_____
_____
_____
_____
_____
_____
_____

Notes:

Page:

Recipe Name:_____

Serves:_____   Cook Time:_____

Ingredients_____   Directions_____

_____
_____
_____
_____
_____
_____
_____
_____
_____
_____
_____
_____
_____

Notes:

Page:

Recipe Name: _____

Serves: _____   Cook Time: _____

Ingredients   Directions

_____

_____

_____

_____

_____

_____

_____

_____

_____

_____

_____

_____

_____

Notes:

Page:

Recipe Name:_____

Serves:_____ Cook Time:_____

Ingredients_____ Directions_____

_____

_____

_____

_____

_____

_____

_____

_____

_____

_____

_____

_____

Notes:

Page:

Recipe Name:_____

Serves: _____ Cook Time: _____

Ingredients _____ Directions _____

_____
_____
_____
_____
_____
_____
_____
_____
_____
_____
_____
_____
_____

Notes:

Page:

Recipe Name:_____

Serves:_____   Cook Time:_____

Ingredients_____   Directions_____

_____
_____
_____
_____
_____
_____
_____
_____
_____
_____
_____
_____
_____

Notes:

Page:

Recipe Name:_____

Serves:_____   Cook Time:_____

Ingredients_____   Directions_____

_____
_____
_____
_____
_____
_____
_____
_____
_____
_____
_____
_____
_____

Notes:

Page:

Recipe Name: _____

Serves: _____ Cook Time: _____

Ingredients _____ Directions _____

Notes:

Page:

Recipe Name:_____

Serves:_____ Cook Time:_____

Ingredients_____ Directions_____

_____
_____
_____
_____
_____
_____
_____
_____
_____
_____
_____
_____
_____
_____

Notes:

Page:

Recipe Name:_____

Serves:_____ Cook Time:_____

Ingredients_____ Directions_____

_____
_____
_____
_____
_____
_____
_____
_____
_____
_____
_____
_____
_____

Notes:

Page:

Recipe Name: _____

Serves: _____ Cook Time: _____

Ingredients _____ Directions _____

_____
_____
_____
_____
_____
_____
_____
_____
_____
_____
_____
_____
_____
_____

Notes:

Page:

Recipe Name:_____

Serves:_____   Cook Time:_____

Ingredients_____   Directions_____

Notes:

Page:

Recipe Name: _____

Serves: _____ Cook Time: _____

Ingredients _____ Directions _____

_____
_____
_____
_____
_____
_____
_____
_____
_____
_____
_____
_____
_____
_____
_____

Notes:

Page:

Recipe Name:_____

Serves: _____   Cook Time: _____

Ingredients   Directions

_____
_____
_____
_____
_____
_____
_____
_____
_____
_____
_____
_____
_____
_____

Notes:

Page:

Recipe Name:_____

Serves:_____ Cook Time:_____

Ingredients_____ Directions_____

_____ _____
_____ _____
_____ _____
_____ _____
_____ _____
_____ _____
_____ _____
_____ _____
_____ _____
_____ _____
_____ _____
_____ _____

Notes:

Page:

Recipe Name:_____

Serves: _____ Cook Time: _____

Ingredients Directions

Notes:

Page:

Recipe Name: _____

Serves: _____   Cook Time: _____

Ingredients   Directions

_____
_____
_____
_____
_____
_____
_____
_____
_____
_____
_____
_____
_____
_____

Notes:

Page:

Recipe Name:_____

Serves:_____   Cook Time:_____

Ingredients_____   Directions_____

_____
_____
_____
_____
_____
_____
_____
_____
_____
_____
_____
_____
_____

Notes:

Page:

Recipe Name:_____

Serves:_____ Cook Time:_____

Ingredients_____ Directions_____

_____ _____
_____ _____
_____ _____
_____ _____
_____ _____
_____ _____
_____ _____
_____ _____
_____ _____
_____ _____
_____ _____
_____ _____
_____ _____

Notes:

Page:

Recipe Name:_____

Serves: _____ Cook Time: _____

Ingredients Directions
_____
_____
_____
_____
_____
_____
_____
_____
_____
_____
_____
_____
_____
_____

Notes:

Page:

Recipe Name:_____

Serves:_____   Cook Time:_____

Ingredients_____   Directions_____

_____
_____
_____
_____
_____
_____
_____
_____
_____
_____
_____
_____
_____
_____

Notes:

Page:

Recipe Name:_____

Serves:_____   Cook Time:_____

Ingredients_____   Directions_____

_____
_____
_____
_____
_____
_____
_____
_____
_____
_____
_____
_____
_____

Notes:

Page:

Recipe Name: _____

Serves: _____ Cook Time: _____

Ingredients _____ Directions _____

_____
_____
_____
_____
_____
_____
_____
_____
_____
_____
_____
_____
_____
_____

Notes:

Page:

Recipe Name:_____

Serves: _____ Cook Time: _____

Ingredients   Directions

Notes:

Page:

Recipe Name:_____

Serves:_____   Cook Time:_____

Ingredients_____   Directions_____

_____
_____
_____
_____
_____
_____
_____
_____
_____
_____
_____
_____
_____

Notes:

Page:

Recipe Name: _____

Serves: _____ Cook Time: _____

Ingredients Directions

Notes:

Page:

Recipe Name:_____

Serves:_____   Cook Time:_____

Ingredients_____   Directions_____

_____
_____
_____
_____
_____
_____
_____
_____
_____
_____
_____
_____
_____
_____
_____

Notes:

Page:

Recipe Name:_____

Serves:_____ Cook Time:_____

Ingredients_____ Directions_____

Notes:

Page:

Recipe Name: _____

Serves: _____   Cook Time: _____

Ingredients _____   Directions _____

_____
_____
_____
_____
_____
_____
_____
_____
_____
_____
_____
_____
_____
_____

Notes:

Page:

Recipe Name:_____

Serves:_____ Cook Time:_____

Ingredients   Directions

_____

_____

_____

_____

_____

_____

_____

_____

_____

_____

_____

_____

_____

Notes:

Page:

Recipe Name: _____

Serves: _____ Cook Time: _____

Ingredients _____ Directions _____

_____

_____

_____

_____

_____

_____

_____

_____

_____

_____

_____

_____

_____

Notes:

Page:

Recipe Name:_____

Serves:_____ Cook Time:_____

Ingredients_____ Directions_____

_____
_____
_____
_____
_____
_____
_____
_____
_____
_____
_____
_____

Notes:

Page:

Recipe Name:_____

Serves:_____ Cook Time:_____

Ingredients_____ Directions_____

_____
_____
_____
_____
_____
_____
_____
_____
_____
_____
_____
_____
_____

Notes:

Page:

Recipe Name: _____

Serves: _____   Cook Time: _____

Ingredients   Directions

Notes:

Page:

Recipe Name:_____

Serves:_____   Cook Time:_____

Ingredients_____   Directions_____

_____

_____

_____

_____

_____

_____

_____

_____

_____

_____

_____

_____

_____

_____

Notes:

Page:

Recipe Name:_____

Serves: _____   Cook Time: _____

Ingredients   Directions
_____
_____
_____
_____
_____
_____
_____
_____
_____
_____
_____
_____
_____

Notes:

Page:

Recipe Name:_____

Serves:_____ Cook Time:_____

Ingredients_____ Directions_____

Notes:

Page:

Recipe Name:_____

Serves:_____   Cook Time:_____

Ingredients   Directions

_____   _____
_____   _____
_____   _____
_____   _____
_____   _____
_____   _____
_____   _____
_____   _____
_____   _____
_____   _____
_____   _____
_____   _____

Notes:

Page:

Recipe Name:_____

Serves:_____   Cook Time:_____

Ingredients_____ Directions_____

_____
_____
_____
_____
_____
_____
_____
_____
_____
_____
_____
_____
_____
_____

Notes:

Page:

Recipe Name:_____

Serves: _____ Cook Time: _____

Ingredients   Directions

Notes:

Page:

Manufactured by Amazon.ca
Acheson, AB